Responsible

Darlene Ryan

orca soundings

Orca Book Publishers

Library and Archives Canada Cataloguing in Publication

Ryan, Darlene, 1958-

Responsible / written by Darlene Ryan.
(Orca soundings)

ISBN 978-1-55143-687-6 (bound)
ISBN 978-1-55143-685-2 (pbk.)

I. Title. II. Series.

PS8635.Y35R46 2007   jC813'.6   C2007-903772-0

Summary: In a new school, Kevin must choose between falling in with a
rough crowd or doing the right thing.

First published in the United States, 2007
Library of Congress Control Number: 2007930151

Orca Book Publishers gratefully acknowledges the support for its publishing
programs provided by the following agencies: the Government of Canada
through the Book Publishing Industry Development Program and the Canada
Council for the Arts, and the Province of British Columbia through the BC
Arts Council and the Book Publishing Tax Credit.

Cover design: Teresa Bubela
Cover photography: Getty Images
Author photo: Kevin Ryan

Orca Book Publishers
PO Box 5626, Station B
Victoria, BC Canada
V8R 6S4

Orca Book Publishers
PO Box 468
Custer, WA USA
98240-0468

www.orcabook.com
Printed and bound in Canada.
Printed on 100% PCW recycled paper.

010 09 08 07 • 4 3 2 1

For Barb and Leigh

Chapter One

See, the thing was, you had to make it look like it was an accident. You know, in case a teacher was looking. Except of course it wasn't an accident, and the person knew it wasn't.

For instance, a couple of us would be walking down the hall, and we'd be talking, and we wouldn't even look at the person. In fact, we'd make a point of *not* looking at the person. Whoever was walking on the inside

1

would bump them—just a little—and we'd keep on going like they weren't even there. And then someone else would come along and nudge them, a little bit harder, but not much. And then it would be Nick's turn.

Nick had a bunch of different moves. The one he liked best was walking down the hall backward, talking real fast to someone, so it really did look like an accident when he banged into the person. But he always hit people hard enough to make them go down. Somehow Nick would end up stepping on their hand or their leg. Once he even stepped on the side of a guy's head, and you could see the shape of the heel of Nick's boot on his face.

Then Nick would go into his big "Oh my God. Jeez, I'm sorry, I didn't see you" routine. A bunch of kids would gather round, and a couple of teachers would come to see what was going on. The whole time Nick kept doing his "I didn't see you" bit. Even though I knew it was all a lie, he was so freakin' good at it that I wanted to believe him.

Mostly Nick got away with stuff because the teachers thought they had him figured out, but they didn't know him at all. One time Ms. Henderson sent me down to the office to bring a couple of boxes of paper towels to the art room. While I was waiting for the secretary to unlock the storeroom, I heard Mr. Harris, the vice-principal, talking to some supply teacher about Nick. He said Nick suffered from low self-esteem and didn't like himself very much.

Teachers, for the most part, don't know anything about real life. If they did they'd have much better jobs than teaching geometry and the history of the stupid middle ages to a bunch of kids who aren't listening anyway. And Mr. Harris knew squat. Nick had low self-esteem? Yeah, right. Nick was the king of cool and he knew it. I'd seen girls checking him out. He even said Ms. Henderson had a thing for him, and I think he might have been right. She did get Nick to pose up on this little platform at the front of the class when we were studying the human form, and she said he had almost perfect proportions.

Nick pretty much always got what he wanted when he wanted it, and I think that's how everything with Erin started. She was about the only person, as far as I could tell, who didn't think Nick was that cool. At least she was the only person who was always in Mr. Harris's office complaining about him. There were other people who didn't like Nick, but they were smart enough not to say anything.

I knew that after the first day in the school. I'd been to a lot of schools— Ellerton was the fourth high school in a year and a half. In my whole life I'd only started and ended the year in the same school twice.

My dad's a carpenter. He can do a lot of other things too, like some electrical stuff and even a bit of plumbing. And he's pretty good, especially for someone who's learned just from watching other people. That was the problem. He didn't go to school to study any of it. Even though he was just as good as trades people with papers, he mostly just got hired as a general laborer.

That meant he'd be one of the first people let go when a job wound down. He had to move around a lot to keep working. Wherever he went, so did I. That's why I'd been to so many schools.

And every school was pretty much the same. There were the brains, the jocks, the techno-geeks in the computer club, the artsy-fartsy types, the drama club kids and the guys like Nick. It wasn't like I'd wanted to hang out with Nick and those guys. It just sort of happened. I learned a long time ago that to survive you had to keep your head down, keep your mouth shut and not make trouble.

But not Erin. She just wouldn't shut up. I don't know why all of a sudden everything Nick did bugged her. They'd gone to the same schools since kindergarten. They had both lived in Ellerton their whole lives.

I heard someone say the whole thing between Nick and Erin was because she wouldn't go out with him. That made sense to me. Nick didn't take no for an answer very well.

So when he *accidentally* knocked her down, it was in the cafeteria and she had a tray full of stuff. There was macaroni in her hair, and butterscotch pudding all down the front of her shirt. Erin got up, and one of her friends started picking macaroni tubes out of her hair. Erin pushed the girl's arm away and moved right in Nick's face. I thought she was going to spit at him. But she just stared at him. Then she turned and walked out of the cafeteria. She never said anything. Of course she went right to Mr. Harris's office. We got a week of detention—Nick because he was the one who'd bumped her, and me, Brendan and Zach because we'd blocked the aisle with our chairs so she'd have to go past Nick in the first place. It was no big deal. My dad was never around after school anyway. All I had to do was sign the note they sent home. That was easy. I could sign my dad's name just as well as he could. I'd been doing it since I was eleven.

Nick made this big deal about being punished for an accident, but Mr. Harris said there'd been too many accidents lately and maybe Nick needed to practice walking around with his math textbook on his head to improve his balance. I thought that was kind of funny, especially coming from Mr. Harris, but Nick was pissed.

On Monday morning there was a chain of tampons hanging down the front of Erin's locker. Nick was in the clear. He always hung out at the Burger Doodle parking lot before school. Probably twenty people or more had seen him there.

On Tuesday, everything disappeared out of Erin's locker at the end of the day.

The day after that she turned on her computer in the tech lab and it started playing "Three Blind Mice" and wouldn't stop. Even Mrs. Woodward couldn't figure out what to do.

I was headed back to my locker at lunch that same day when Nick suddenly came up beside me. "Hey, man, I need you to do something for me," he said.

Crap. My mouth suddenly got all dry. Whatever it was he wanted, I knew I couldn't say no. "What is it?" I asked.

Nick leaned on the wall by the water fountain. "I can count on you, Frasier, right?" he said.

"Yeah," I said. I wasn't stupid enough to get into a pissing contest with Nick. He pulled a Styrofoam hamburger box out from under his jacket.

"Here," he said. I took the box and started to open the cover. "Don't open it," Nick hissed. "Just put it away."

I shoved the box in my backpack. I didn't know what was in it, but I was pretty sure it wasn't Nick's leftover lunch.

"Remember that Erin chick?" Nick said.

I nodded. A burning feeling started in my stomach.

"She thinks she's better than us, yuh know? Going around with her nose in the air and trying to get people in trouble all the time. You do that and stuff's gonna happen."

The burning filled my stomach.

Nick grinned. It wasn't nice. He looked at my pack. "That's just a little pet for

Miss Perfect. All you gotta do is wait till no one's around after school and put it in her locker. You know how to pop a lock, right?"

I knew. The locks were so old they'd probably been using them back in the days when Mr. Harris had gone to the school. It was easy to force one open and lock it again.

"Wait till everyone is gone and watch out for the janitors," Nick said. He slugged my shoulder. "She's gonna freak. Thanks, man." He took off down the hall.

I walked to my locker and frigged with the lock, waiting until the hall cleared. I grabbed the burger box and shoved it behind some books on the top shelf. I didn't look inside. I didn't want to know what was in there until I had to.

Chapter Two

At the end of the day I slipped the box back into my backpack and went down to the art room. I knew I could hide out there for a while, pretending that I was working on a sketch of a tree I was doing for my art project. I figured since I had to be there I might as well do a bit more work on the trunk. On paper it didn't look the way it did in my head.

Ms. Henderson walked by the door. When she saw me she came over to the table. She picked my half-open backpack off the chair and set it on the floor so she could sit down. I thought I was going to pass out, but she didn't notice anything.

"That's nice work, Kevin," she said. "You have real talent." She smelled like turpentine and oranges. Ordinarily I would have been happy—really happy—to have Ms. Henderson leaning over me with her elbows on the table and her orange-smelling hair about an inch from my face, but all I could think was, Don't let her look in my backpack. We weren't allowed to have fast food on the school grounds. If she saw the box, she'd take it, and while I wasn't exactly sure what was inside, I knew it wasn't a cheeseburger with extra pickles.

But she didn't even look down. She just pointed to a couple of places in the picture that she thought needed more detail, and then she got up. As she walked away I could hear the blood pounding in my ears.

After half an hour I put everything away and went up the back staircase. The hallway was deserted. I found Erin's locker. The lock was easy to pop, even with the sleeve of my sweatshirt pulled down over my fingers. I didn't think Mr. Harris had any way of looking for fingerprints, but I wasn't taking any chances. I slid the burger box out of my pack.

There was a mouse inside, gray and black with a long hairless tail and blood, dried brown, on its neck. I looked at it, curled in the bottom of its Styrofoam coffin, and I thought, I could just shut Erin's locker and tell Nick I hadn't been able to pop the lock after all. No. No. I could tell him the janitor had been doing the floors and I couldn't even get to her locker.

I looked down at the grungy gray and yellow tiles. Nick wouldn't believe that. No one would believe that.

I could just shut the locker, throw the box in the garbage and go home. Of course I'd never be able to come to school or go anywhere else ever again. I'd heard rumors about what Nick did to guys who went up against him. I was pretty sure I wouldn't get a mouse like this stuck in my locker. I'd probably be the mouse, curled up in a ball with blood on the side of my head. It was me or her. What the hell else could I do?

I hauled my sweatshirt down over my fingers again and picked up the mouse. I had thought it would be stiff, but it was as floppy as a stuffed toy. I set it on Erin's math book, right at the front of her locker, so she'd at least see it first thing. That way she wouldn't be feeling around for her books and get a handful of dead rodent instead. She was going to freak no matter what.

I felt like the mouse was looking at me, sitting there on the middle shelf of the locker. A cold shiver rolled from my shoulders all the way down my back. "Sorry," I whispered as I closed the locker door. I wasn't sure if it was for the poor dead mouse or for Erin.

I couldn't get going in the morning, so by the time I got to school it was almost first bell. Nick was standing at the bottom of the main stairs with Zach and Brendan and some geeky kid from grade nine who talked way too much. I thought his name was Oliver. I knew Nick was just hanging there, waiting to see what happened when Erin opened her locker.

I walked over to them. I just wanted to go to my locker or homeroom, but it would have looked weird if I had. I didn't look down the hall. We'd know soon enough when Erin opened her locker.

Nick was going on about video games and playing *Doom Master.* He thought he was hot stuff because he'd gotten to level six in the game. I'd gotten as far as level fourteen. That wasn't something I'd ever told him, though.

I didn't see Erin until she was right behind Nick. "Uh, Nick," Zach said, pointing. I looked around. It seemed like half the school was hanging around, watching. I wondered if Nick had put the word out.

Erin was holding the mouse up by its tail with her bare hand. If she was scared,

I couldn't tell. In fact, she was sort of smirking. "Jeez, Nick," she said. "I thought you could come up with something better than a dead mouse."

Then she reached over and stuffed the mouse in the pocket of Nick's Zipperhead T-shirt. "Here you go," she said, giving the pocket a pat. Yeah, she was definitely smirking.

Nick jerked. He grabbed the mouse out of his pocket and hurled it down the hall. It landed with a splat by the water fountain. He wiped his hand on his jeans. He was breathing hard and there was sweat on his forehead. Erin wasn't afraid of a dead mouse, but Nick sure as hell was.

I bit the inside of my cheek so I wouldn't laugh, but I could hear snickers all around me. Everyone was watching Nick. I thought he might hit Erin, but at that moment Mr. Harris came down the steps. Erin moved in front of him. "Mr. Harris, Nick put a dead mouse in my locker—probably after school yesterday."

My ears burned.

Darlene Ryan

"I didn't put anything in your locker yesterday," Nick said. "Or any other day."

Erin didn't even look at him. She took a step closer to Mr. Harris. "There was a dead mouse in my locker this morning. You know about all the other stuff. When are you going to do something about it?"

"Where's the mouse?" Mr. Harris asked. Erin pointed toward the fountain. "Don't move, any of you," Mr. Harris said. He walked down the hall, stared at the dead lump of gray fur and walked back. "Erin, this is an old building," he started to say.

She didn't let him finish. She waved her hand in front of his face. "No, no, no. Don't try to tell me this was just some poor mouse that somehow crawled into my locker by accident and died right on top of my math book. No! How did it get in there? What was it? The David Blaine of mice?" She looked at Nick then. "No, he did it."

Mr. Harris took a slow deep breath—it was probably a technique he'd learned at vice-principal school. "I don't know how a

16

mouse got in your locker—they can squeeze through amazingly small cracks—however, I know Nicholas didn't put it there. He was in detention with me yesterday afternoon and again this morning."

Nick gave Erin a smug smile, like a cat that had just swallowed two or three fat mice.

Erin bit her lip and let out a breath. "Then it was one of the toadies that walk around kissing his ass." She pointed at Zach. "That one." She turned and jabbed her finger at Oliver. "Or that one. Why do you put up with his crap? Why the hell don't you do something?"

"I am going to do something," Mr. Harris said. He had almost no lips, I realized, kind of like a salamander. And his bald head had the same kind of knobby shape. "I'm giving you detention for the next three days. You can use the time to think about what kind of language you should be using in this building."

"This is ridiculous," Erin shouted. Her face was almost the same color as the crimson hockey championship banner hanging from the ceiling. "That jerk harasses me for weeks, puts a dead animal in my locker, and I get detention. This place is insane."

Mr. Harris did his deep-breathing thing again, and then he held up three fingers. "Want to make it four days?" he said. Erin pressed her lips together. I figured she was probably biting her tongue too. She looked at Nick. All I could see was hate on her face, hard in her eyes and tight mouth. She turned and walked away.

Mr. Harris turned to Nick. "It would be best if you stayed away from Erin," he said. "And I don't want to find out you or any of your friends had anything to do with this."

"You won't, sir," Nick said. I don't know how he managed to keep a straight face. Me, I just stared at my feet and wished I was invisible.

Chapter Three

Nick waited until Mr. Harris had disappeared down the hall and around the corner. I hoped Erin getting detention would make up for her making him look stupid with that mouse.

He ran his hand back over his hair. "So Miss Prissy-Ass is getting detention. I'm not sure that'll teach her the lesson she needs to learn."

"What're we going to do?" Brendan snickered. Mr. Harris may have looked like a salamander, but Brendan looked like a ferret. There was an old guy in the trailer park who had one. He took it for walks on a leash, just like a dog. That's what Brendan looked like—a pointy face and tiny ears—except the ferret could grow more hair on its face than Brendan could.

Why did we have to do anything, I wondered.

"What did you say?" Nick said.

Crap! I'd said it out loud.

"What did you say, Frasier?" Nick asked again.

I was screwed. He was moving slowly, talking quietly, like a snake, waiting to strike. I had to say something.

"Why should we do anything? I mean, why even bother with her anymore?" I tried to grin but my mouth wouldn't cooperate. "You got her sent to detention. Isn't that enough?"

Nick slammed me against the stone wall under the stairs before I even knew what was happening. "I'll decide what's enough," he hissed. "You saw what she did, putting that frickin' mouse in my pocket. You think some stupid detention makes that okay?" He was holding me by the throat, and it was hard to breathe.

"No," I managed to choke out. My mouth was filling with spit, but I couldn't swallow. "I just...I just didn't think...she was worth...worth it." Nick's thumb and finger were digging into the sides of my neck so hard his face was beginning to wobble and shimmer in front of me.

Then suddenly he let go and I sank to my knees. "Here's a hint, Frasier," Nick said. "Don't think. You might hurt something." He leaned over me. "And keep your mouth shut. Got it?"

I nodded. Nick straightened up and headed down the hall. The other guys followed him without saying a thing. Slowly I got up. My throat felt like the time I'd had strep throat when I was eight, but at least all my limbs were still attached to my body and there wasn't any blood anywhere.

Nick made a big production of leaving Erin alone for the rest of the day. If they came near each other in the halls he'd hold up his hands and back against the wall. "Look. I'm staying out of your way," he'd say, but there was a mocking tone to his voice and a sarcastic smirk on his face. Erin just walked past as if he was invisible.

I tried staying out of Nick's way too. In gym when we played dodgeball—and who came up with that stupid game anyway?— Nick pretty much pounded me with the ball every chance he got, and I let him. He didn't just have to get even for what I said. He had to get ahead, and everyone had to see it. By the time the class was over there were bruises coming out on both my arms, and my ribs on the left side ached every time I took a breath. Nick slapped me on the back as we headed for the showers. "Your timing sucks, Frasier," he said with a grin. "You oughta work on that."

I didn't like it when Nick was so happy. It always meant he had a plan. He wasn't just going to get even with Erin. He was going to do the same thing he'd done with me—get ahead.

That night I stood at the stove making Kraft dinner and hot dogs, wishing for once that my dad was home. The whole left side of my chest was a giant red and purple bruise that hurt when I moved, when I breathed, when I did anything.

I took my bowl over to the little table jammed in against the wall. I looked around as I ate and suddenly realized my dad's guitar was gone. Not his precious '54 Les Paul Goldtop, but his regular one. That meant he was out playing somewhere and wouldn't be home till maybe one or two o'clock. Dad would probably tell me it served me right for hanging out with those guys in the first place. He would say, "Why do you hang around those punks? Stay out of things that aren't your business? Don't go looking for trouble."

But I couldn't stay out of things. Okay, I didn't exactly go looking for trouble, but

I did look for Erin, Monday after school. Well, I sort of looked for her. I really did need to do some more work on my tree project, so I spent about an hour in the art room after school, and it was Erin's last day of detention. I took the trail along the river because I knew that's the way she walked. Sometimes I walked home that way, even though it took a bit longer, and I'd seen her ahead of me on the gravel path. When I came out of the trees, there she was.

I had to run to catch up with her. Erin jumped when I touched her shoulder. She turned and took a step back. "What do you want?" she said, holding her bag to her chest with both arms.

What did I want? I stumbled over the words. "I just…I just wanted to tell you…to warn you to…watch out for Nick."

"Are you threatening me?"

"No!" I held up my hands. "Jeez, I swear, no. I just…you shouldn't trust him. Just be careful."

She studied my face. "Why? What did he say?"

"He didn't say anything." I jammed my hands in my pockets. "I'm tryin' to help you here. You've known him way longer than I have. You know what Nick's like. He's not going to let this thing between you just die."

She shrugged. "If you're so sure he's going to do something then why don't you go to Mr. Harris, or even the police?"

"Going to Mr. Harris didn't do you much good, did it?" Did she have to be so difficult when I was only trying to help her?

"That's because no one else will speak up," Erin snapped. "No one will say anything. You're all a bunch of mindless sheep. Everyone is so damn afraid of him. Well, I'm not afraid. If he tries something, he'll be sorry."

She stalked away, still holding her bag to her chest, her shoulders hunched. I didn't bother going after her. I could taste something sour in my mouth. I knew for sure that whatever Nick did, he wouldn't be sorry about it—but Erin would.

Chapter Four

On Friday morning, I was getting my books when Nick came up and leaned against the locker beside mine. He smiled. It made me think of one of the trailer park cats, George, a big ginger missing most of an ear. George got the same look on his face that Nick had, though when the cat looked that way there were usually a few feathers poking out of his mouth.

Nick punched my arm right on one of

my fading bruises. I sucked in a breath and swallowed my gum trying not to yell.

"Hey, Frasier, you spend a lot of time in the art room, right?" he said.

"Yeah," I said slowly.

He leaned closer, and the smile got more George-like. All he needed was a dark gray pigeon feather sticking out of the corner of his mouth. "And Ms. Henderson's there, right?"

"She's around," I said.

Nick looked over his shoulder and then back at me. "See, I've got this little bet going with McCarthy that Ms. Henderson doesn't wear a bra. I figure today after school, when you're working on your little project, you're going to need some up-close and personal help. You can do a buddy a favor and report back what you see, you know what I mean?"

"Umm, yeah, sure, I can do that."

"After school today, okay?" he said.

"Yeah, all right." I nodded.

"Perfect." Nick slugged me again and took off down the hall.

It was the only thing I could think about all day. I was going to have to look down the front of a teacher's blouse and see what kind of underwear she had on. Thinking about maybe seeing a woman's breasts should have been exciting, but it wasn't. This was Ms. Henderson. I knew a lot of the guys thought she was hot, but I liked her, I mean as a teacher.

After school I went to the art room and got my tree poster out. I didn't know what I was going to say to get Ms. Henderson into the room, but I didn't have to do anything. She just came in to see how I was doing, and when she leaned over I looked.

"It was a purpley-colored thing with lace," I told Nick and the guys. They'd been waiting for me out on the picnic tables. "Like a slip or something."

Nick nodded. "Nice work, Frasier." He looked at Brendan and jerked his head toward the street. "We gotta go."

I knew he didn't mean me. I watched them walk across the grass, laughing, and somehow I knew the whole thing had been a setup. Since when did Nick get someone else to look at someone's boobs—even a teacher's? He was always checking Ms. Henderson out. He'd just wanted to see if I'd do it. I wasn't one of the guys, not like Brendan or Zach. They'd all been friends since first grade, back when Nick was swiping the fruit rollups out of other kids' lunchboxes and looking up the girls' dresses from under the swings. Me, I didn't really belong. Never did.

When I got home, the car was parked next to the trailer. My dad was sitting at the table inside. "What are you doing home?" I said. "The job can't be done yet. You said there was at least six more months of work."

He ran his hand across the back of his neck as though his shoulders hurt or something. "Yeah, well, the job's done for me," he said. "I got fired."

"What do you mean you got fired? What for?"

"Remember I told you I was gonna sell

some stuff—you know, a couple of saws and that cordless drill—so we could make the rent on time?"

"Yeah."

"One of the air nailers is missing from the job site. I was using it yesterday. Then somebody saw me selling stuff out of my trunk last night…"

"You told them you didn't steal it, right?" I threw my bag on the floor by the table and opened the fridge, looking for something to drink.

Dad leaned back in the chair and stuck his feet out under the table. "'Course I did. But I can't prove it."

I twisted the cap off a bottle of root beer and took a gulp before the brown foam spilled over the side. "And they can't prove you took anything," I said.

"Well, it doesn't work that way. I've been working on that job for three months. The guy who saw me selling stuff out of my car has worked for the company for twelve years. Who you think they're gonna believe?"

"That sucks!"

"Yeah, I sort of pointed that out to the foreman." He rubbed the back of his right hand, and for the first time I noticed his knuckles were bruised.

"You didn't punch him out, did you?" I said.

He half grinned at me. "Naw. I did this on the driver's door of the car." Then his face got serious. "But I did take a swing at the fat old fart. I was pissed off and I didn't think. Lucky for me a couple of guys stopped me. It coulda been a lot worse than just me getting fired."

I looked down at my running shoes. There was a small hole in the right one. It didn't seem likely I'd be getting new ones any time soon. "So we'll just move," I said. "So what?"

Dad looked around the trailer. "Don't you ever get tired of moving, Kev?" he asked. "Wouldn't you like to stay in one place for more than a few months? Maybe...maybe even live in a house instead of a tin can?"

Sure I would have liked to live in a house and be in the same school at the end of the year as I had been at the start. Like that was gonna happen.

I shrugged. "I don't care." I finished the root beer, tipped the bottle on its side and set it spinning. "Your boss is a jerk," I said.

Dad nodded. "Yeah, but so was I, and I'm the one without the job, not him."

He reached across the table and his hand came down on the twirling bottle. "You're going to stay in school, and when you graduate you'll learn how to do something. Hell, maybe you'll even go to college."

"Right, me in college," I said. "There's a laugh."

"I don't know how the hell I'd pay for it anyway," Dad said. "But you're getting some kind of education. You want to go from one crap job to another the way I have my whole life? That's no life, believe me."

He got up, opened the refrigerator and grabbed the last root beer, but instead of opening it he just stared at it for a minute and then put it back. He grabbed his jacket off the back of the chair. "I'm goin' out for a while. Get yourself something to eat and do your homework."

Chapter Five

I was dead asleep when Dad came into my room and shook me awake. "Get up," he said. "Your old man's gonna be on TV."

I stared at him, only half awake, with drool running down from the corner of my mouth. It had to be almost midnight.

"C'mon," Dad said. I staggered down the tiny hall to the front room of the trailer. Dad turned on the TV and used the remote to flip through the channels. "I hope we didn't miss it," he muttered. Suddenly, there was my father's face on the screen. I yanked the remote out of Dad's hand and upped the volume.

"There was more than three thousand dollars in the envelope," a chirpy blond reporter was saying. "Did you ever think about keeping the money, Mr. Frasier?"

"No," the TV Dad said. "It wasn't mine. It wouldn't be right."

I looked at my dad—the real one. "You found a bunch of money?"

"Yeah," he said. "Close to four thousand dollars in the middle of the street, right outside of Greer's junkyard. I took it to the police station."

I thought about what four thousand dollars could buy—running shoes without a hole in them; something, anything besides Kraft dinner and hot dogs; somewhere else to live other than this tuna can on wheels. I shook my head. "Four thousand freakin' dollars just sitting in the middle of the street and you take it to the cops. Hello? You don't have a job. We can't even pay the rent this month."

35

He didn't look at me. "It wasn't my money," he said quietly.

"It was in the middle of the street," I said. "It wasn't anybody's money. Did you at least get a reward?"

Dad slowly pulled a fifty from his pocket.

"Oh, that's sweet. That won't even buy groceries," I said. "I'm going back to bed."

Dad wasn't home when I got up in the morning. The Les Paul was there, but the other guitar was gone. I had the last of the cornflakes—dry because there wasn't any milk—and half the orange juice. Then I put some cheese slices in my pocket—the kind wrapped in plastic—and went outside to sit on the steps. In a few minutes Penelope peeked around the side of the Jensens' place. As soon as she was sure the coast was clear, she bolted across the grass strip between the two trailers, scampered up the steps and hopped onto my lap. She tapped the pocket of my jeans with a front paw.

"Hang on, you little mooch," I said. She started to purr. I pulled out a cheese slice, peeled off the plastic and fed her little bits while I stroked her black fur. She might have looked like a sleek black panther, but Penelope was about as menacing as a teddy bear. Suddenly her head came up and her ears started twitching. She bolted down the stairs and across the space between the two trailers in a flash.

George was on the way. Somehow Penelope always knew. A couple of minutes later he came strolling down the middle of the chip-sealed road like a lion crossing a dusty African plain. He climbed the steps and sat down beside me. After a moment he butted my arm with his head. I unwrapped the other two cheese slices and fed them to him while I scratched behind his one ear. Then we sat there in the sun for a while, watching the world go by.

George was Charlie Hetherington's cat. Charlie and my dad were friends. Charlie was sort of the trailer park caretaker. That meant when there was trouble, Charlie would stop by your place and pretty soon you'd be wishing you'd kept your mouth shut, your pants zipped or your hands to yourself.

Dad claimed Charlie had won George in a poker game along with a 1972 El Camino and a case of beer with one bottle missing. Dad also said George and Charlie were a lot alike. I suppose they were, as much as a big ginger cat with one ear and a big bald dude with half a middle finger on his right hand could be.

After a while George decided he had things to do. He gave me another head butt and wandered away. I thought I'd go for a walk. I locked the trailer, cut around the back of the park and got on the trail. Charlie said that years ago there had been railroad tracks all over, but there hadn't been trains around for years. Most of the tracks had been dug up and replaced with gravel walking trails—the "green" solution.

I wandered up behind Sloppy Joe's Takeout. I checked the pockets of my jean jacket. Nothing. I didn't even have enough for an order of small onion rings.

There were a few benches, a couple of garbage cans and a beat-up picnic table on the strip of grass behind Sloppy Joe's. Oliver, the twerpy grade nine kid who had started hanging out with Nick and the others, was sitting by himself on top of the table, eating a burger. I walked over to him. "Hey," I said.

"Hey, Kevin," he said with a mouth full of cheese and meat. He really was a twerp.

There was a small plate of onion rings beside him on the table, the grease already soaking into the cardboard. I took one without asking. They were just the way I liked them—hot and greasy.

"I thought you'd be getting ready," Oliver said. "You know, for later." He reminded me of a puppy, all eager and twitchy.

I grabbed another onion ring. "What do you mean?"

He looked all around—not that there

was anyone else there but us. "I know what you guys are going to do tonight," he said, and I swear to God his tongue was hanging out just a little bit.

If my mouth hadn't been full I probably would have asked what the hell he was talking about. But I couldn't talk for a second and that was just enough time for my brain to catch up. He knew what Nick had planned, but I didn't. But how did he know? There was no way Nick had said anything. He wasn't that stupid.

"Yeah, well that's not till later," I said. "How did you know, anyway?"

Score! His face got all red and he looked down at his feet. "Don't say anything to Nick, okay?" he whined. "You know I can sort of get around those controls they put on the library computers, so you can't play games and stuff? I was overriding the program—it's not that hard to do—and Nick was standing there talking to Zach and Brendan about that girl, Erin." Oliver glanced up at me. "I have really good hearing. Really. I got tested and everything, and I can hear stuff when other people can't—"

I cut him off. "And you heard what Nick said."

He nodded. "I haven't told anyone. I wouldn't."

Right. Except here he was telling me.

I glared at him. At least I hoped that's how it came across. I was bigger than he was, and I could pound him if I had to, but I didn't want to. "What did you hear?"

Luckily he was the kind of person who talked way too much. He put the last bit of his burger on the paper wrapper and wiped his hands on his jeans. "Not that much, really. I know that you're going to be waiting for her on the trail after she gets off work and take her down into the woods behind the school." His voice was so damn whiney I thought I might have to pound him after all.

I kept on eating the onion rings, like I wasn't all that interested in what he was saying.

"And…and I heard Nick say about her

hair. How you're gonna shave it off and all." He laughed. "She's gonna have to go to another school or get a wig or tie a scarf around her head the way people who have cancer do."

Nick was going to shave Erin's head. How did he think he was going to get away with that?

"Go," I said to Oliver. "Go home and keep your mouth shut. You got it?"

He nodded. Then he took off. He was afraid of me. He didn't even stop to grab the rest of his food. Yeah, I was such a tough guy. Except now what was I supposed to do? Go tell Erin? Oh yeah, that had worked so well the last time I'd tried it. Try to stop Nick? I thought about how it still hurt when I took a deep breath. No way.

What made him think it would work, anyway? Even if they could grab Erin without her seeing them, she'd know their voices. She'd know because who else would want to do something like that to her? Did he think she wouldn't go to the cops?

It wasn't going to work. She'd see them or hear them and run and scream and it wouldn't work.

I gathered up the garbage and stuffed it all in one of the cans. Then I went home.

Chapter Six

Dad was back. He'd had a haircut and he smelled like some kind of aftershave that made my nose prickle. He was standing in front of the little closet, going through his shirts. His guitar was back in its usual place. "Where were you?" he said.

"Out," I said, dropping into a chair. "Where were you?"

He looked over his shoulder at me. "Out," he said, mimicking my voice.

"At Rusty's," I said. Rusty's was a bar near one of the highway off-ramps. They were always after my dad to play there. He was good, and he knew all the old country and rock stuff people wanted to hear. But it's kinda hard to be in a bar and not drink a lot, and it was better if he didn't drink too much. I don't mean that he got rough or anything. He'd just cry and miss my mom and be depressed for weeks. So it was better if he didn't go to Rusty's at all.

His back stiffened. "Yeah, I was at Rusty's. We got rent due, and I like to eat." There was silence for a moment and then he continued, "I didn't drink. Not even one." He found the shirt he was looking for and pulled it on.

"Nice haircut," I said, sarcastically. It was a lot shorter than Dad usually wore his hair, but it looked okay. Not that I'd tell him that.

He grinned. "I'm being interviewed for the newspaper. Not that little rinky-dink one here—the morning paper that goes all over everywhere. It's one of those 'do the right thing' stories." He shrugged. "Maybe something'll come of it."

Do the right thing. What was the right thing when it came to Nick and Erin? "Dad, can I ask you something?" I said.

He was rooting in the closet again. "What?" he said.

How could I say it? I know this guy who's going to drag this girl into the woods and shave her head?

Dad straightened up, holding his leather jacket. "I don't have a lot of time, Kev."

"When I was out I was talking to one of the guys from school and—"

"Not the one who 'accidentally' hit you a dozen times playing that stupid game in your gym class?" I'd blamed all the bruises I'd gotten from Nick—even the ones on my neck—on the dodgeball game. I hadn't been able to hide them.

"No, not him. It was one of the guys he hangs with and—"

"How many times I gotta tell you? Stay away from those guys!"

I leaned across the table. "No, see, Dad, you don't understand—"

But he wouldn't let me finish a sentence. "Just stay the hell away from them. Why is that so hard?" He was still going on as he pulled on his jacket. "Christ! If those morons all ran off the side of a cliff, would you go over right along with them? You've got a brain. For once in your life, use it. Can't you find someone else in that school other than those punks to be friends with?"

"You don't get it," I said.

Dad held up his hand and cut me off. "I don't want to hear your excuses. Just stay away from them." He jerked his head in the direction of the refrigerator. "Your supper's in there. I don't know what time I'll be back." Then he was gone.

I slumped down in my chair. What could I do? I'd tried everything. And what was the worst that could happen? So they shave her head, I thought. It's just hair. It will grow back.

Chapter Seven

There was coleslaw and fried chicken in the fridge. I saved some of the meat for the cats and ate everything else. Then I played *Doom Master* for a while, but I couldn't get past level eight.

Maybe Dad was right, I thought. Maybe it would just be better if I stayed away from Nick and those guys for good. Anyway, if Dad didn't find a job soon, we'd be moving again. And then none of it would matter.

I found half a bag of bacon-flavored chips in one of the cupboards. They were kind of stale, but I ate them anyway.

It wasn't that big a deal. It was just hair. Nick would make her look stupid, and then he'd be happy and start torturing someone else. And it wasn't like I hadn't tried to warn Erin about Nick. Besides, maybe Oliver had everything wrong. Just because he was a geekazoid didn't mean he was smart.

I looked at the clock over the sink. It was eight o'clock. I knew Erin worked at the Pumpkin Patch, and it closed at eight. The potato chips felt like a big greasy lump in my stomach.

What if I just walked over there? Oliver said they were going to take her into the woods behind the school. I hadn't grown up in Ellerton, but I knew the woods and the trails pretty well just the same. I could find them, sneak up and see what was going on without getting caught.

I could hear my dad in my head saying, "Stay away from them." But I couldn't stand it. I'd just go see what they were doing. Nothing else. I couldn't think about it anymore. I grabbed my sweatshirt, locked the trailer and took off.

It wasn't hard to find them. I ducked into the woods at the edge of the football field and walked slowly, watching the ground and listening. I heard them before I saw them. They were in a bit of a clearing surrounded by thick cedars and alders. I crouched beside a twisted tree trunk.

All three of the guys were wearing coveralls—the disposable kind painters sometimes use. That made sense. Nick's uncle was a painter. And they were wearing Halloween masks: a cartoon mouse, a dog and a duck.

I looked for Erin. She was on her side on the ground. My stomach rolled over and I tasted something sour in the back of my mouth. She was blindfolded with a rag and tied up with duct tape. All she was wearing was jeans, sneakers and a bra. I saw what I figured was her shirt—it was orange, the color the staff wore at the Pumpkin Patch—thrown to one side near the trees.

I edged a little closer, staying low to the ground until I was just a few feet away. Nick was making fun of Erin's underwear, just a plain white cotton bra—no lace, nothing sexy. I knew it was Nick, but not just because he was the tallest of the three. It was the way he stood, like he owned the world.

"I shoulda guessed you were some kind of lesbo," I heard him say. He was using a voice distortion box that made his voice sound mechanical, like he was some kind of machine. The coveralls, the masks, the voice thing—he'd done a lot of planning. I tried to swallow the sourness in my mouth, but it wouldn't go away.

Erin tried to sit up, but Nick pushed her back down with one foot. "Where you goin'? The party hasn't even started yet."

They'd cut off her braid. Ragged bits of hair hung down to her chin. An ugly welt on the side of her face was already turning purple. There were streaks of dirt on her jeans. I squinted at Nick and noticed a long scratch on the back of his left hand. Erin had to have done that. Good for you, I thought.

"I know it's you, Nick," she said, lifting her head a little. "You're wasting your time with your little Robo-Ranger walkie-talkie." She kicked her feet out. "And I know that's you, Zach. I can smell your aftershave from here."

Nick turned toward the cartoon duck and held up a warning hand.

"And you're here too, Brendan. You always smell like gas. Maybe that's why you can't get a girl to stand near you."

The dog mask started for Erin, but Nick stepped forward and stopped him. Then he kicked Erin's feet. "Shut up," he said in the mechanical voice.

Erin sucked in a sharp breath. "And I know you, Nick, because I can smell the stink of trash anywhere."

Shut up, Erin, I thought. Just shut up. Let them shave your head and get it over with.

Nick bent over and grabbed Erin by the jaw, pulling her up so she was sitting. She was shaking. Nick traced his index finger down the side of Erin's neck and along the top of her shoulder, pushing her bra strap down at the same time. There was a smirk on his face, and I could hear how hard he was breathing. He pushed his mask up onto the top of his head.

My stomach sloshed like I was on the Spinmaster at the Exhibition. Nick ran his finger across Erin's throat. Something in the way he was touching her, playing with her, reminded me of George playing with a bird he'd caught one time.

The cat had come wandering up the road with a tiny finch in his mouth. I thought the thing was dead, and I was going to take it away from George, get a shovel and bury it. Then the cat dropped the bird onto the grass. It started to flap its wings. George reached out with one big orange paw and gave it a smack. After a minute he lifted his paw and started washing his face. The finch tried again to get away. George paused long enough to bat it down and went back to washing behind his good ear. The bird didn't move again. When George finished, he poked the bird a couple of times with a paw. Then he picked it up, came across the lawn to the driveway and dropped it at my feet. He looked up at me and I swear he had the same smug grin I could see on Nick's face.

Nick had pushed down Erin's other bra strap and trailed his finger down along her collarbone.

I can't let him do this, I thought. What time was it? Would there be anyone in the school at this time of night? Could I run to the school, find help and get back in time?

I wished I'd stayed home, stayed away like my dad had said. There wasn't anything I could do. There were three of them and one of me. Nick could hurt me all by himself and then do anything he wanted to Erin. How was that going to help her?

My legs were shaking. I looked at Erin with Nick looming over her. She was so close I could almost touch her myself. She was crying, not making any sounds, but

I could see the tears soaking the bottom of the blindfold. Zach and Brendan stood there watching Nick—just as Erin had said—like sheep.

Maybe I could talk to him. Maybe I could make Nick see that if he went any further it was going to seriously screw up his life. Maybe I could talk Erin into keeping her mouth shut and then everything would be all right for everyone.

Maybe Nick would turn me into roadkill.

Chapter Eight

I got to my feet and stepped out from behind the trees.

"What in hell are you doing here?" Nick said. He didn't even bother with the voice changer. "You didn't see anything. Go home."

I shook my head and pressed the palms of my hands against my thighs so my legs wouldn't shake so much. "You don't want to do this, man," I said. "C'mon, let it go. It's not worth it."

Two steps and Nick was inches away from me. "How would you know what I wanna do?" he said. Bits of spit hit me in the face. "You think you're my mother or something?" Nick shoved me with both hands, and I went down on my knees. Erin had started to crawl away, even though she couldn't see.

Nick moved in front of her and stepped on her hand. She screamed. "You're not going anywhere," he said. "We haven't had our little party yet."

I struggled to my feet and shoved Nick aside. "Leave her alone."

He laughed. "You're telling me what to do, pussy? Get your ass out of my way and get your own girlfriend."

"She's not your girlfriend," I said. "Walk away, Nick." I tried to make my voice stronger. "You can't do this. It's gone way too far. Leave her alone and get out of here. It's not too late." I glanced down at Erin. "Nobody is going to say anything. Right?"

Nick smiled and gave an elaborate shrug.

"Well, I wouldn't want to go too far," he said. He turned as though he was going to leave. Then he whipped back around and punched me square in the gut.

I dropped like my legs had been chopped off. Nick kicked me in the ribs, the left ones that were still bruised. It was like a knife slicing through my chest. I couldn't breathe.

Nick bent over me. "Listen to me, you little freakin' pussy. Nobody tells me what to do." He looked over his shoulder at Erin. His voice suddenly sounded slimy. "Don't worry, sweet stuff. I haven't forgotten about you," he said. "We'll have our little party in a minute."

He yanked me up by the front of my sweatshirt, half choking me. I looked at Zach and Brendan in their stupid masks, just standing there. "Help me," I croaked. They didn't move. Nick punched me in the face, and then he smashed me across the mouth. He let go and I slumped to the ground.

I tasted blood. Everything in front of my

right eye went blurry. Nick kicked me in the ribs, again and again. I kicked at him, but I couldn't make contact.

Erin was screaming. Nick looked at Brendan. "Shut her up." For a second, Brendan hesitated. "Shut her up."

Brendan leaned over Erin and pressed his hand hard over her mouth. She bit him. He pulled his hand back, swore and slapped her. "She bit me!" he yelled.

Nick's arm shot out, and he grabbed Erin by the hair. "You're gonna be sorry for that," he told her. "Very sorry."

She spat at him, catching the side of his chin. Slowly he wiped the spit away with the sleeve of his coverall. Then he slapped Erin so hard her head whipped to the side.

"Cops are coming," I croaked.

Nick laughed again. "God, you are so freakin' stupid. You expect me to believe you called the cops? If you had, they'd have showed up, not you."

"My dad." Blood was filling my mouth. I turned my head to spit. "I left a note.

My dad…home from work by now. He'll call…for sure."

"Yeah, you left a note for Daddy, pussy boy. Sure you did." Just then, miraculously, I heard sirens.

For a second I thought I was hallucinating. Then I saw Nick's face, and I knew the sound was real. "Told you," I whispered. I needed Nick to take off before he figured out the sirens were going somewhere else. "I didn't…no one knows your name…go and you're out of it."

The sound was getting louder.

Nick gave me one last kick to the back of my legs. "We're not done, pussy boy," he said. He pulled Erin to her feet.

No! I tried to get upright, tried to speak, but there was blood in my mouth again. "Let's go," Nick said to Erin. "Time to move the party."

Erin turned her head and puked all over Nick. "Christ," he shouted. "You freakin' bitch!"

The sirens seemed to be getting closer. Were they coming to save us?

Nick stripped off his coveralls and rolled them into a ball.

"C'mon," Brendan said, pulling at Nick's arm. "We gotta get out of here."

Nick hesitated, and then he bent over me. "You are going to be so goddamn sorry," he said. I held my breath. I could hear something nearby in the trees—was it my imagination? Was it help? "Go," Nick said to Brendan and Zach, and they all took off into the woods.

I rolled onto my side and heaved too. Erin crawled over to me, feeling her way along the ground. "The police will be here in a minute," she said.

"No police," I choked out.

"What do you mean?"

"Made it up. Got to…get out of here." I tried to sit up but the trees started swirling around me.

"Are you all right?" Erin said.

"I don't…know." I leaned against her and managed to sit up. I reached over and pulled down her blindfold. My arm accidentally brushed her shoulder and she jerked away. I fell back down, groaning with pain.

"I'm sorry," Erin whispered. "I didn't—"

"S'all right." I got on my side and managed to sit up without her help. For a minute I just took deep breaths and the swirling slowed down.

"Stick out...your arms," I said. Erin looked at me, confused. "Arms." Then she got what I meant. She turned her back to me and stuck out both arms.

I managed to pull off the duct tape. She whimpered when the last bit came loose from her skin.

"Sorry," I whispered. Erin peeled the tape off her ankles. I got my right arm out of my sweatshirt, but I couldn't lift the left arm over my head. I couldn't take a deep breath because the pain was so bad on my left side. There was no way I could pull the shirt off by myself. "Help me," I said to Erin.

"What are you doing?" She pulled back again and wrapped both arms around herself. She was still shaking.

I was sticky with sweat and not so sure I wasn't going to barf again, but I had the polar fleece half off. "Help me," I said again.

Erin hauled the sweatshirt over my head. I used the hem of my T-shirt to wipe my face and looked down for a second at my partly bare chest. Erin stared wordlessly at the red welts and dark bruises already forming.

"Put it on," I said, pointing at the sweatshirt. "I didn't puke on it." The sirens suddenly stopped. Erin stared down at the gray fleece in her hands. "Put it on. We gotta get out of here. They might come back."

Slowly she pulled the shirt over her head.

"I'm sorry," I told her. "You're gonna have to help me get up."

"You need a doctor," she said. "I think something's broken."

"Just help me get up."

I bit my tongue hard so I wouldn't scream, and somehow I got to my feet. For a moment my vision darkened. I grabbed

Erin's arm and tried to breathe more slowly. The darkness faded away.

"This way," I said. I knew there was a makeshift path through the woods that would bring us out by the school and the football field. I kept hold of Erin's arm and we stumbled along in the dark. A branch whipped against my cheek. I hoped we were going in the right direction. I listened for the sound of people, of sirens again, of anything but Nick and the others coming back.

Suddenly Erin tripped and I went down too. It took me a minute to get my breath again. "I'm sorry. Are you okay?" Erin asked.

I turned my head and spit blood again. Then I nodded. Erin pulled me upright and put my arm over her shoulder. We started moving again.

"Why now?" Erin asked suddenly. "Before, you didn't do anything to stop them. You were one of them. I don't get it."

Up ahead, finally, I could see light and hear people. I looked at Erin, wondering if

I was going to puke or pass out before we made it the last few feet through the woods. "I don't know," I said, because I didn't.

Chapter Nine

By the time my dad got to the hospital, I'd been X-rayed, had a bunch of blood taken and been more or less cleaned up. I was sitting on the edge of the stretcher, talking to one of the police officers who'd shown up at the school. The father of one of the kids who'd been playing flag football at the field had called 911 on his cell phone. A few minutes later and they would have all been gone. Turns out the sirens we'd heard were headed to a fire at Sloppy Joe's. So we were saved by greasy onion rings.

I heard Dad's voice in the hallway, asking where I was. Then he was standing in the doorway. "Christ, Kevin," he said, shaking his head. "I thought you knew better than to be fighting. What the hell were you thinking?"

That was my dad. Yell first, get the facts later. The veins were sticking out in his neck, which meant he was majorly pissed and only holding in his anger because there was a cop there. The officer stood up and stepped between the stretcher and my dad.

"Mr. Frasier, your son wasn't in a fight. He was beaten up when he stepped in and prevented a girl from being sexually assaulted."

"What?" Dad said.

The police officer glanced over his shoulder at me. "I don't like to think what might have happened if your son hadn't been around."

Dad just stood there, silent, for a long

moment. Then he said, "The girl. Is she all right?"

Way to go, Dad. Don't ask if I'm all right.

"She's being examined, but as far as we can tell, yes, she's all right. Your son has some pretty bad bruises, but the doctor says nothing's broken."

Dad walked over to the stretcher. "Kev, I'm sorry," he said, quietly. He laid his hand, lightly, on the top of my head for a moment before I pulled away. "Who did this to you?" Dad asked.

"Some guys from school," I said. I stared at the pink tile floor instead of him.

"You know who these guys are?" Dad asked the officer.

"We're looking for them, and there are cars at their homes. It's a small place. We'll find them."

"And then what? What are you going to do to protect my son and the girl?"

"Mr. Frasier, I have a fourteen-year-old daughter," the police officer said. "I don't want those punks walking around any more than you do."

The nurse came in to put a bandage on my head. Some guy who hadn't looked old enough to be a real doctor had put stitches in the cut by my ear. "The doctor will be in to talk to you," she told Dad. "We're waiting for the ophthalmologist to check his eye."

My right eyeball, the one Nick had punched, was blood red. That side of my face, around the eye, was purple and getting darker.

Dad took hold of my face with one hand and turned it so he could have a look. "Jesus," he muttered. He glanced at the nurse. "Sorry."

"I know it looks bad," she said. "But I'm pretty sure it's okay. Come in here any Sunday morning and you'll see worse."

While we waited for the doctor, I finished answering the police officer's questions. I left out the part about trying to talk to my father. The officer promised to be in touch. "You did good," he said to me. The eye doctor walked in as he was leaving.

Darlene Ryan

My eye was fine, or at least it would be, was the doctor's verdict. It wasn't going to swell up and explode, and I wasn't going to go blind. He told me to make an appointment to see him at his office in a week and left.

Dad was leaning against the wall with his arms crossed. I shot a quick glance at him, and then he looked away again. I heard him swallow a couple of times.

"I am sorry," he said finally. "I shouldn't have assumed the worst. I should have asked."

The nurse had given me some pills earlier. They made me feel kind of numb. Mostly I felt like I didn't care. "Forget it, Dad," I said. "What else is new? You always expect me to be the screwup, don't you? Sorry to disappoint you this time."

The same nurse came back with a prescription and handed it to Dad. I heard her say something about how often I should take the pills and what side effects to watch for. "Bring him back Tuesday to have the dressing changed on that cut," she said.

"My, uh, friend. Erin. Is she okay?" I asked. I hadn't seen Erin since the police had arrived at the field.

"She's already gone home." The nurse smiled at me from the door. "I think you're a very brave young man," she said. "Take care of yourself."

I managed to get down off the bed by myself. "Here, let me help you," Dad said. He grabbed my clothes off the back of the chair.

"I can do it," I said. Dad laid my stuff on the end of the bed. I picked up my pants and managed to pull them on using just my right arm. I even got the zipper up. But I couldn't get my T-shirt on. I couldn't even get it over my head.

Wordlessly, Dad took the shirt away from me. He tugged it over my head and eased my arms into it. Even with the stuff they'd given me for the pain, the room swam in front of my eyes for a second when he lifted my left arm.

"Is this all you were wearing?" Dad asked.

I figured Erin had taken my shirt home with her. "Yeah, that's it."

Dad was still holding the paper the nurse had given him. "We can't afford that," I said.

"Let me worry about it," Dad said.

Charlie's car was squeezed in at the end of a row of parked cars, half on the grass and half on the pavement. I figured that meant our car wasn't running again. We drove home without talking. Dad watched the road and I looked out the side window.

Back at the trailer I was so tired it was all I could do not to fall over. I peeled off my jeans and got into bed. Dad came in and handed me a couple of pills and a glass of water. "Take them," he said.

"Where did you get those?" I asked. My mouth felt fuzzy.

"The nurse gave them to me to get you through until I can get that prescription filled."

"I don't need them."

"Take them."

"I don't want them."

"Just take the goddamn pills," Dad snapped. "For once do what's right for you instead of trying to figure out how you can screw with me."

I swallowed the capsules and drank half the glass of water.

"I'm going to get some food and get that prescription filled," Dad said. "Charlie is gonna come over until I get back."

"I don't need a babysitter," I protested. It was hard to keep my eyes open.

"If those guys come looking for you, I want someone here who can break some heads," Dad said. I wasn't awake enough to argue anymore.

Chapter Ten

When I woke up it was light outside. Everything hurt. My ribs, my face, my teeth, even my hair. But it was a different kind of pain—the sharpness was gone. I didn't know if that meant I was healing or that the pills were still floating around in my bloodstream.

It probably took me five minutes just to get out of bed, but I did it. I managed to pull on a pair of sweatpants that looked fairly clean. I had to hold on to the wall on the way down the hallway, but I made it out to the front room of the trailer.

Dad was leaning on the counter by the sink, nursing a cup of coffee. There were dark circles under his eyes, his hair was standing up and he had on the same clothes as the day before. He stretched as though he was trying to work out a kink in his back. I managed to make it across the floor to the table without anything to hold on to. I dropped into a chair. I was breathing harder than if I'd just run all the way around the trailer park.

"Hey," Dad said, "how do you feel?"

"Okay," I muttered.

"You look like crap."

"Gee, Dad, you sure know how to make a guy feel better," I said.

Dad came over to the table and tipped my head back so he could look at my eye. "Some of the red is gone."

"See, I told you it was okay."

"You still have to go back and have it checked. Don't even think about not doing that."

I didn't say anything.

Dad crossed over to the fridge. "What do you want to eat?" he asked.

"What is there?" I said. "Let me guess. Cornflakes or puffed wheat."

Dad pressed his lips together, looked away from me for a moment and then back. "I got stuff for pancakes," he said, "and syrup—the real thing, not the stuff that's just all sugar and colored water."

"Wait. You're going to make me pancakes?"

"Sure."

"I guess I should get the crap beaten out of me more often. I can't remember the last time you ever made anything for me except maybe a can of beans."

"It's not funny," he said, pulling things from the fridge. "Those punks could have killed you."

"Yeah, well, they didn't. You always said I had a hard head. I guess you were right about that." My head felt like there was a pinball game going on inside it.

"Why didn't you tell someone?" Dad said.

"Who?" I snapped. "Mr. What-does-the-school-guidebook-say Harris? The cops? Right. Like they would have done anything. You, Dad? You were too busy being the poster child for Honesty Week."

"You're right," he said in a low voice. "I messed up royally, and I'm sorry, but things are going to change around here. I'm going to change."

"Yeah, right." I couldn't help it. I gave a snort of laughter, and then I sucked in a breath because it hurt.

Dad looked at me without saying anything. Then he turned back to the pancakes.

We ate breakfast in silence. I looked at my distorted reflection in the toaster. The bruises on my face went from red to purple with some black in places. There was a big bandage by my ear, covering the stitches.

"You did the right thing," Dad said suddenly.

"So if it's the right thing, how come I had to have part of my face sewn back together?"

"I didn't say it was the easy thing. I said it was the right thing."

"Oh, yeah. I forgot I'm talking to Mr. Honesty, Mr. TV Celebrity. So are you getting your own TV show, Dad? Am I going to see your face on the side of a bus with 'Do the right thing' written underneath?"

"Cut the bull," Dad said. "All I did was return something that didn't belong to me. I didn't go looking for those reporters. They came looking for me."

"I didn't see you hiding, Dad."

He didn't answer at first. He stared at me, and I could see his jaw tighten as he ground his teeth together. "Yeah, you're right, Kevin. I didn't hide. Like you said before, I don't have a job anymore." He kicked at my sneakers with the toe of his boot. "You can forget about new sneakers. I don't have the money to get the car fixed. I don't have the money for next month's rent. So I figure, yeah, maybe somebody sees me on TV. Maybe they think there's an honest guy and they offer me a job."

"That worked real well."

His hand moved, and I thought for a second he was going to smack me one. But he didn't. He cracked his knuckles instead. Then all of a sudden he reached down and grabbed me by the arm. "Stand up."

A rainbow of swirling colors swam in front of my eyes. "Hey, what did I do?" I said.

"Stand up," he said again, pulling me to my feet.

I bit the inside of my cheek to keep from making any noise. There was no way I was going to let him know how much it hurt.

He dragged me into the bathroom, which was barely big enough for the two of us, and we stood in front of the sink. "Look at yourself," Dad said.

I took a quick look at my beat-up face.

He put his hand on the back of my head and forced it toward the mirror. "Look. At. Yourself."

I tried to twist away, but he had his other hand on my arm, holding on so tight I could feel his fingers squeezing through my shirt. The pain went up a couple of notches. I could feel the sweat on my scalp, and for a second I thought I was going to puke pancakes on his boots. He might have been the same size as me, but he was stronger and I was one giant bruise. I looked down at the grubby sink. There were still little bits of hair and foamy soap in it from him shaving.

He let out a breath. "You know what I did when I found that money, Kevin?" he said.

"Yeah, the whole freaking town knows what you did with it. You took it to the police station because it wasn't yours."

"No," he said in a low voice, and then he let go of me.

For a second the little room whirled around me like I'd twisted myself around and around on a swing and then let go and gone spinning in the opposite direction. I grabbed the edge of the sink with both hands.

"I put it in my pocket and I took the car over to Melanson's to get it fixed."

I looked at him then. "You did what?"

"There was no name. No wallet. And there was enough money to get everything done so the car would pass inspection. There was enough to pay next month's rent and to buy groceries—something other than cornflakes, Kraft dinner and powdered milk." Now it was him who couldn't look at me.

"So the whole thing was a fake." I pulled my voice lower and mimicked him. "Oh no, I never considered keeping the money." Where did he get off lecturing me about doing the right thing? "You freaking phony." I started out of the bathroom, but his hand shot out and caught the neck of my shirt.

"But I didn't get the new brakes and tires for the car. I didn't pay old man Barton the rent." Now he was looking at me. "I went to the police station and I turned in the money."

"But you almost didn't."

"Yeah, and my stomach felt like I'd drunk a bottle of toilet bowl cleaner. I wanted to be able to look at myself in the mirror every morning when I shaved and not be ashamed." Dad let go of my shirt. "I told you, Kevin. The right thing is not the same as the easy thing." He pushed past me and went back into the kitchen.

Chapter Eleven

I stood there, hanging onto the doorframe until my stomach settled and the pain slid down a couple of degrees. Then I wobbled back to my chair. There was half a cold pancake floating in syrup on my plate, but I didn't feel like eating anymore. Dad stood at the counter with his back to me, hands wrapped around a coffee cup. "The right thing doesn't always get you money and a parade, Kev. Sometimes all it gets you is a fifty and a handshake. Sometimes you get worse."

There was a knock at the door of the trailer. Dad looked over at me. "Don't move," he said. I couldn't have if I'd wanted to.

He opened the door. A blond man with jeans and a dark blue sweater was standing there. He didn't live in the park, and his hair was too long for him to be one of the holy rollers out to save our souls. We got a lot of them around the park.

"Mr. Frasier?" the man said. "I'm Michael Tennant. Erin's father."

"Erin?" Dad said. Then he got it. "The girl that…"

Erin's father nodded and offered his hand. "Yes." They shook hands.

"Could I talk to you for a moment?" Mr. Tennant asked. "It won't take long."

Dad stepped back. "Sure, c'mon in."

Crap! I wished he didn't have to see the inside of the trailer. Not that the outside was so impressive.

"How's your daughter?" Dad asked.

"She's all right, because of your son." He turned to look at me, swallowing as he studied my face. "Thank you, Kevin, for everything you did for Erin." He shook his head. "I had no idea he'd been this badly hurt."

"I'm all right," I said. "It just looks... bad." I sounded lame.

Mr. Tennant pulled an envelope out of his pocket.

Dad shook his head. "No."

What did he mean, no? The guy hadn't done anything.

"Mr. Frasier, I just want to say thank you. When I think about what could have happened..." He didn't finish the sentence. He didn't have to.

"You have said thank you," Dad said. "We can't take your money."

What was this *we* stuff? The man had been about to give *me* the money. Not Dad. And I could take his money. Going by his clothes, he wasn't exactly broke.

Mr. Tennant looked at Dad. "Wait. You're the guy who was on the news. You

found all that money and gave it back."
Dad nodded. "What do you do?" Erin's
dad asked.

"I can do just about anything," Dad
said. "But mostly construction. I've been
looking for a job. The last one I had was
just...temporary. I'm looking for something
a little more permanent."

"I know quite a few people around this
area," Erin's father said. "If you won't let
me give the boy any money, at least let me
ask around, put in a good word, maybe find
you something."

Dad hesitated. Don't blow this one off,
I thought. "Thank you," he said, finally.
"I...I'd appreciate that."

They shook hands again. "If he needs
anything, please let me know," Mr. Tennant
said, inclining his head toward me.

"Thank you."

As he turned to go I blurted, "Please
tell Erin...tell her I'm sorry and I hope
she's okay."

Erin's dad smiled. "She is. Thanks to
you." Outside, on the steps of the trailer,

he stopped. "Erin isn't going back to that school. I'm having her transferred into the next district. If you want to do the same thing and they give you any hassle, you let me know."

"We will," Dad said. He came back in and picked up his coffee cup.

"Why didn't you let me have the money?" I asked.

"Is that why you helped that girl? For money?"

"No, but—" I didn't get a chance to finish.

"Is that why you got the crap pounded out of you?"

"No."

Dad put down the cup and folded his arms across his chest. "You did what you did because it was the right thing. Not the easy thing. Not the safe thing. And not to get paid."

I wasn't sure I'd done what I'd done because it was the right thing. I'd helped Erin because, in the end, I couldn't not help her. Was that what doing the right thing meant? And did it make it any less right if I took that money? Erin would still be safe and I'd still be black and blue.

"I'm not going to another school," I said. If I couldn't have the money, then he couldn't make me switch schools. "I'm not running away like a girl."

"You like being a punching bag?" Dad said. "You want to lose that eye for real?"

"Those guys have probably been arrested by now. They're not going to be in school."

"Yeah, but their friends are."

I struggled to my feet and started toward my room. "Nick's a jerk. No one will feel bad because he's gone. I'm not going somewhere else."

"We're not finished," he called after me.

"Yeah, we are," I said as I closed the door. I didn't know if he'd heard me, and I didn't care.

Chapter Twelve

The bruises changed color a little every day. Every morning, Dad went out looking for work. I spent most of my time hanging around the trailer. Charlie checked in three or four times a day. I slept a lot, played *Doom Master* and sat outside with the cats. I thought a lot about Erin.

Finally I couldn't stand it any longer. In the phone book I looked up where she lived. Dad kept a bunch of maps in the car.

I drank half a carton of milk that night at supper so we'd be out. When he left to walk down to the convenience store, I went out to the car, found the map with Ellerton on it and looked for Erin's street.

It wasn't even that far away. I figured Erin probably hadn't started her new school yet. She had bruises too. I knew once Charlie checked up on me after lunch the next day I'd have at least an hour before he came back. Charlie never missed *The Young and the Restless*.

And that's how it went. As soon as Charlie was gone, so was I. I was stiff, but I didn't mind the walk. I hadn't exactly figured out what I was going to do or say when I got to Erin's house. I stood at the bottom of the driveway, wondering if I should just walk up to the door and ring the bell, when I saw her come around the side of the house with a big black dog. I started up the driveway, and the dog began to bark. I saw Erin freeze. Then she saw it was me. She called the dog and held it by the collar. "You're a good boy," I heard her say, patting it on the head. I stopped at the edge of the lawn. "What are you doing here?" Erin said. Her hair had been cut short and sort of fluffy. It looked good.

The dog had stopped barking. It sat beside her, watching me. I got the feeling it would be quite happy to use my leg for a chew toy.

"I...I wanted to see if you're okay."

"Well, now you've seen me and you can see that I am," she said.

Jeez, what was the matter with her? "Why are you so pissed off?" I said.

"Oh, how should I be, Kevin? Should I be grateful, is that it? Or am I supposed to feel sorry for you because you got your face kicked in?"

"Hey, I helped you. Nick could have... you know."

"So? One time you did the right thing. Do you think that makes up for all the times you were one of them? For the times you stuffed dead things in my locker and spread rumors about me? Well, guess what? I don't want to be your friend, and if you think I'm going to get all stupid and weepy over you saving me, well, forget it. You're still a jerk."

I opened my mouth but nothing came out. I didn't know what to say. I shoved my hands in my pockets, turned and walked away.

The next morning there was a plastic grocery bag hanging on the trailer door. Inside was my sweatshirt, washed and folded.

Chapter Thirteen

After a week at home, I was going a little crazy. I just didn't care that much about *The Young and the Restless*—although I wasn't dumb enough to say that in front of Charlie. Dad gave in on me going back to the school. Nick and the guys were gone. I figured a lot of people were probably happy about that.

The second I stepped in the building, I knew something was wrong. I could feel people looking at me, but it was like I smelled or something—no one came near me.

At lunchtime I found *Snitch* had been sprayed on my locker in fluorescent pink paint. Inside, a dead rat hung from the shelf with a little noose around its neck. There was a sticky note stuck to its chest with *Kevin* written on it. I wanted to run. Nobody cared what Nick had tried to do to Erin. All they cared about was that I had told. I'd done the right thing and it didn't matter. Not to Erin. Not to anyone. I wasn't even getting fifty bucks and a handshake. I was getting squat.

I got a bag of chips from one of the machines instead of going to the cafeteria. It was cold outside, and it looked like it was going to rain. I went out anyway and sat on one of the big rocks close to the football field, away from the school and away from the picnic tables. I ducked my head down and pulled my jacket around me, wondering if I should just go home.

All of a sudden I was swarmed by a group of kids, mostly guys, but some girls too.

My heart felt like it was going to come out of my chest, it was pounding so hard. I got to my feet.

"You don't know how to keep your mouth shut," someone said.

Then someone else said, "Tattletales belong in kindergarten. You should learn to stay out of things that aren't your business." Someone pushed me. Then someone else. They shoved me back and forth. I struggled to keep my balance and stay on my feet.

"Look, just leave me alone," I said. I took a sucker punch in the stomach that knocked the wind out of me. I doubled over, wheezing.

"What's the trouble," someone sneered. "Is the rat having trouble breathing?"

Just then a loud voice said, "Knock it off." Several kids looked around. "I said knock it off."

It was my dad. Charlie was with him in his shades and a sweatshirt with the sleeves cut off at the elbows. You could see his tattoos and his muscles.

"Get the hell away from my son," Dad said. He pushed his way through the group and put his hand on my back.

"You heard the man," another voice said. It was Mr. Harris. He called each of the eight or nine kids around me by name and said, "Report to my office now." A couple of the guys started to complain. "Stuff it," he said. "Both of you. I don't want to hear it right now. All I want to see are the backs of your heads moving toward my office."

They started straggling across the grass. I'd gotten my breath again and straightened up. Dad kept his hand on my back. Charlie hadn't moved so much as a muscle.

"Are you all right?" Mr. Harris asked.

I nodded.

He turned to Dad. "Mr. Frasier, I apologize. You were right. You have my word I'll deal with this."

"Yeah, well, no offense," Dad said, "but your word isn't worth much to me right now." He put his arm around my shoulders. "We're going home." We started for the front of the school.

"You knew something like this was going to happen," I said.

"I guessed."

"What were you doing? Watching the school from the time I got here?"

"More or less. Me. Charlie. Couple of kids Charlie knows inside." Charlie smiled at me, just a little.

The car was at the curb. "How did you get the car fixed?" I asked.

"I sold a couple of things," Dad said.

"What things?"

"Oh, some blood, a kidney, you know, nothing serious." He tossed the car keys to Charlie, who still hadn't said a word.

We went to the drive-thru at Burger Doodle and took the food back to the trailer. "Thanks," Dad said to Charlie.

"Not a problem." He took the bag with his two double cheeseburgers. "It's almost time for my show. Let me know if you need anything else."

It wasn't until I'd finished eating that I noticed the Goldtop was gone. "Dad, where's your guitar?" I asked.

"It's right there."

"No," I said. "The Goldtop. Where is it?"

"I sold it," he said, not meeting my eyes.

"Sold it? What do you mean, sold it? Why?"

He looked up at me then. "We needed the money."

"We've been broke before and you never sold it."

Dad looked at me for a long moment before he answered. "Yeah, well, maybe that was my mistake," he said at last.

"You love that guitar."

"You're more important than a guitar. Even that guitar."

I swallowed a couple of times because for a second I almost felt like crying. "Well, when we get some money we'll just go get it again."

He shook his head. "I didn't hock it, Kev. I sold the guitar to a collector. It's gone."

"But…" I couldn't finish the sentence.

I didn't know why I cared. I couldn't play the stupid thing. I didn't even like it.

Dad put his hand on my shoulder. "In the end it's just a guitar. I can get another one."

"But not like that one."

"It's a guitar. Wood and lacquer," Dad said, his voice suddenly hoarse. "There are thousands, millions of guitars in the world. You're one of a kind."

A week later I was starting at a new school in a new district. Dad had a new job as well, thanks to Erin's dad. On the weekend we were moving, away from Ellerton, into a real house. A small one that needed a lot of work. But still, it wasn't a trailer.

The first day was like every other first day of school in my life. Nobody talked to me, the teachers couldn't remember my name and I was way behind.

At lunch I took my tray to the end of a vacant table at the back of the cafeteria. I was just starting to eat when a voice said, "Can I sit here?"

I looked up. Erin stood there with her tray. She had red streaks in her hair. They looked good. For a long moment we stared at each other. "Uh. I'm growing roots here," she said.

"Oh, um, yeah, sit down," I said.

She took the chair next to me, arranged her food and picked up a fork. "Can you believe all this healthy crap? I mean, no French fries?"

"Yeah," I said. "And who eats vegetarian pizza?"

Erin gestured at the potatoes on my plate. "It helps if you get extra gravy," she said.

"I'll try to remember that," I said. Then she smiled at me and started to eat, and I thought maybe, just maybe, we were doing the right thing.

Darlene Ryan has been writing since she figured out that letters made words and words made stories. *Responsible* is her third book from Orca Book Publishers, following *Saving Grace*, another Orca Soundings novel, and *Rules for Life*, a YALSA Teen Top Ten and a Best Book nominee.

Darlene lives in Fredericton, New Brunswick. Visit her web site at www.darleneryan.com

Orca Soundings

Bang
Norah McClintock

Battle of the Bands
K.L. Denman

Blue Moon
Marilyn Halvorson

Breathless
Pam Withers

Bull Rider
Marilyn Halvorson

Bull's Eye
Sarah N. Harvey

Charmed
Carrie Mac

Chill
Colin Frizzell

Crush
Carrie Mac

The Darwin Expedition
Diane Tullson

Dead-End Job
Vicki Grant

Death Wind
William Bell

Down
Norah McClintock

Exit Point
Laura Langston

Exposure
Patricia Murdoch

Fastback Beach
Shirlee Smith Matheson

Grind
Eric Walters

The Hemingway Tradition
Kristin Butcher

Hit Squad
James Heneghan

Home Invasion
Monique Polak

House Party
Eric Walters

I.D.
Vicki Grant

Juice
Eric Walters

Kicked Out
Beth Goobie

Orca Soundings

My Time as Caz Hazard
Tanya Lloyd Kyi

No More Pranks
Monique Polak

No Problem
Dayle Campbell Gaetz

One More Step
Sheree Fitch

Overdrive
Eric Walters

Refuge Cove
Lesley Choyce

Responsible
Darlene Ryan

Saving Grace
Darlene Ryan

Snitch
Norah McClintock

Something Girl
Beth Goobie

Sticks and Stones
Beth Goobie

Stuffed
Eric Walters

Tell
Norah McClintock

Thunderbowl
Lesley Choyce

Tough Trails
Irene Morck

The Trouble with Liberty
Kristin Butcher

Truth
Tanya Lloyd Kyi

Wave Warrior
Lesley Choyce

Who Owns Kelly Paddik?
Beth Goobie

Yellow Line
Sylvia Olsen

Zee's Way
Kristin Butcher

Visit www.orcabook.com for all Orca titles.

Orca Currents

Camp Wild
Pam Withers

Chat Room
Kristin Butcher

Cracked
Michele Martin Bossley

Crossbow
Dayle Campbell Gaetz

Daredevil Club
Pam Withers

Dog Walker
Karen Spafford-Fitz

Finding Elmo
Monique Polak

Flower Power
Ann Walsh

Horse Power
Ann Walsh

Hypnotized
Don Trembath

Laggan Lard Butts
Eric Walters

Manga Touch
Jacqueline Pearce

Orca Currrents

Mirror Image
K.L. Denman

Pigboy
Vicki Grant

Queen of the Toilet Bowl
Frieda Wishinsky

Rebel's Tag
K.L. Denman

See No Evil
Diane Young

Sewer Rats
Sigmund Brouwer

Spoiled Rotten
Dayle Campbell Gaetz

Sudden Impact
Lesley Choyce

Swiped
Michele Martin Bossley

Wired
Sigmund Brouwer

Visit www.orcabook.com for all Orca titles.